For Adrian – JD

For Anna and Emily – LM

First published 2013 by Macmillan Children's Books
This edition published 2018 by Macmillan Children's Books
an imprint of Pan Macmillan
20 New Wharf Road, London N1 9RR
Associated companies throughout the world
www.panmacmillan.com

ISBN: 978-1-5098-6266-5

Text copyright © Julia Donaldson 2013
Illustrations copyright © Lydia Monks 2013

3 5 7 9 8 6 4 2

A CIP catalogue record for this book is available
from the British Library.

Printed in China.

SUGARLUMP and the Unicorn

WRITTEN BY
JULIA DONALDSON

ILLUSTRATED BY
LYDIA MONKS

MACMILLAN CHILDREN'S BOOKS

The unicorn has a silver horn,
Her eyes are bright and blue,
And when she hears a horse's wish
She can make that wish come true.

Sugarlump was a rocking horse.
He belonged to a girl and boy.
To and fro, to and fro,
They rode on their favourite toy.

"Here in the children's bedroom
Is where I want to be.
Happily rocking to and fro.
This is the life for me!"

But when the children were out at school
Sugarlump hung his head.
"Oh to be out in the big wide world!
I wish I could trot," he said.

"Done!" came a voice, and there stood a beast
With a twisty silver horn.
"I can grant horses' wishes,"
Said the snow-white unicorn.

She pawed the ground and tossed her mane
And flashed her eyes of blue.
Seven times she turned around,
And the horse's wish came true.

Now Sugarlump was a farmer's horse,
Pulling his cart and load.
Clippety-clop, clippety-clop,
He trotted along the road.

"Here in the open countryside
Is where I like to be.
Clippety-clop, clippety-clop,
This is the life for me!"

But time went by and the hills grew hard.
Sugarlump hung his head.
"Oh to be free of this heavy load.
I wish I could gallop!" he said.

"Done!" came the voice of the unicorn,
And she flashed her eyes of blue.
Seven times she turned around,
And the horse's wish came true.

Now Sugarlump was a racing horse
With a jockey on his back.
Gallop-a-jump, gallop-a-jump,
They thundered down the track.

"Here on this famous race course
Is where I like to be.
Gallop-a-jump, gallop-a-jump,
This is the life for me!"

But time went by and the jumps grew hard.
Sugarlump hung his head.
"Oh to slow down and have some fun!
I wish I could dance," he said.

"Done!" came the voice of the unicorn,
And she flashed her eyes of blue.
Seven times she turned around,
And the horse's wish came true.

Now Sugarlump was a circus horse
With his tail tied in a bow.
Dancing and prancing around the ring,
The star of every show.

"Here in this splendid circus
Is where I like to be.
Dancing and prancing, prancing and dancing,
This is the life for me!"

But time went by, and the children's cheers
Made Sugarlump hang his head.
"Oh for a child to ride me!
I want to go home," he said.

"Done!" came the voice of the unicorn,
And she flashed her eyes of blue.
Seven times she turned around,
And the horse's wish came true.

Sugarlump was a rocking horse,
But where were the girl and boy?
Time had flown and they both had grown
And forgotten their favourite toy.

Alone in the attic, Sugarlump sighed,
"I wish I had never been born!"

"But I have a better wish for you,"
Came the voice of the unicorn.

She pawed the ground and tossed her mane
And flashed her eyes of blue.
Seven times she turned around
And – the unicorn's wish came true!

Now Sugarlump is a fairground horse
On a beautiful merry-go-round.
Merrily up he rises
And merrily down to the ground.

"Here in this fabulous fairground
Is where I love to be.
Merrily, merrily, round and round,
This is the life for me!"

So Sugarlump is a happy horse.
The children are happy too . . .
And the unicorn with the silver horn
Closes her eyes of blue.